## Battle of the Bad-Breath Bats

# Read more 13th Street books!

HARPER **Chapters**

# Battle of the Bad-Breath Bats

## by DAVID BOWLES

### illustrated by SHANE CLESTER

**HARPER**

*An Imprint of* HarperCollins*Publishers*

To my cousins Kristi Pérez and Joseph
Casas, for all the secret adventures. —DB

# CONTENTS

# CHAPTER

# BAD DREAMS AND BREAKFAST

In the dream, Malia kept running and running. She was trying to beat the dark shadow that had blocked the sun. Something was coming for her. A cold wind blew her hair into her face.

Then the smell of fresh tortillas and the sound of music woke her. Opening her eyes, Malia looked around the unfamiliar pink room.

It took her a second to remember where she was.

Aunt Lucy's apartment in the Little Mexico neighborhood of Gulf City was much cooler than her family's home in the sleepy town of Nopalitos.

She was spending the whole summer here. "Yes!" she whispered. She grabbed her cell phone from the nightstand and went to the living room.

"Oh, great. Almost forgot." She sighed at the two boys still asleep on the sofa bed. Her cousins, Ivan and Dante. Unfortunately, *they* were spending the summer with Aunt Lucy, too.

"Hey, goofballs!" Malia said. "Get up already!"

Dante groaned. "Yes, boss."

"You've got to be kidding." Ivan yawned.

"Shouldn't have stayed up late playing video games," Malia said.

"That was me," Dante said. "Walking brain here was reading a book."

"And you were texting your friends, Malia," Ivan said. "Don't judge."

She rolled her eyes and walked away. The boys followed behind her.

The kitchen was colorful, full of clay pots and copper pans from Mexico. The music Malia had heard was coming from a little speaker on the counter. It was a *cumbia*, a happy, upbeat song. Aunt Lucy danced to the rhythm as she cooked.

The last flour tortilla puffed up, steaming. Aunt Lucy grabbed it, spun around dramatically, and dropped it onto a plate.

"Good morning, sleepyheads!" she exclaimed. "Ready for a late breakfast and some summer fun?"

Malia smiled. "Yes, please!"

The three of them sat at the table as Aunt Lucy served, singing the song under her breath.

"Uh, what's in the eggs?" Ivan asked.

"Onion, tomato, chorizo," Aunt Lucy replied.

"Chorizo?"
Ivan seemed
confused.

"It's sausage."
Dante chuckled.
"He's not all that
Mexican, *tía*."

Ivan's face went red. "Not cool, Dante."

"Don't be embarrassed, *m'ijo*! We'll fix that soon enough!" Aunt Lucy winked at Ivan and he smiled.

Thankfully, it turned out that Ivan liked chorizo just fine. The cousins ate everything on their plates. Orange juice helped wash it all down.

"Okay," Aunt Lucy said, clapping her hands together. "There's a neighborhood water park. Super close. Lots of fun stuff to do there. Pool, hot tub, high dive, and . . . a water slide!"

Ivan sat up straighter. "How tall?"

Aunt Lucy stretched her arm to the ceiling. "Crazy tall!"

Dante gulped. "Um, sounds dangerous."

"But you need to hurry to beat the crowds," Aunt Lucy said.

Ivan and Dante raced each other to the bathroom. Malia changed in the guest bedroom. In a flash they were ready, waiting by the front door.

"Now, it's not far," their aunt said, giving them detailed directions. "The slide rises up above the sign to the water park. Can't miss it!"

"Wait," Dante said. He sounded worried. "You're not coming?"

"Oh, no, cutie. I've got a bunch of work to do. You three can handle this. Right, Malia?"

"Yes!" her niece replied.

They hurried out the door. Malia blinked. The sun was shining. The day was already getting hot.

Then, out of nowhere, a cold gust of wind blew Malia's hair into her face.

She shivered, remembering her nightmare.

# CHAPTER

# A SHADY SHORTCUT

Malia turned to her cousins, holding up her hand.

"Listen up, boys. I'm the oldest, so I'm in charge. Follow my lead."

Ivan smiled. "You're two months older than me. Big deal. I'm taller and smarter."

"Whatever." Malia turned to Dante, who was shorter and . . . not as smart. Still, sometimes he acted a little stuck-up. "Any problem?"

Dante shrugged. "Nope. You're the boss. He's the brain."

Ivan laughed. "What does that make you?"

"The beauty, of course," Dante replied.

"Come on, slowpokes. We're wasting time," Malia said.

Off they went. Ivan had decided to wear **ALL** his swimming gear because he liked to be prepared. "I'm ready!" he shouted.

Dante grinned. "Time to show off these hazel eyes in the hot tub."

Malia sighed at her weird cousins.

As they headed down 11th Street, she patted the head of her yellow duck floatie. "I'm going to float all afternoon. When I'm not speeding down the slide, I mean."

"Hello, children!" a sweet voice exclaimed. It was an old woman, sweeping the sidewalk in front of a little house. "You must be new to Little Mexico."

"Yes, ma'am. We're visiting our aunt for the summer," Malia replied politely.

The old woman's eyes twinkled. "Going to the water park, I see."

"Yes," Ivan said.

The old woman glanced at Malia. "Why carry a purse, *m'ija?*"

"It has my phone and other important stuff in it," she answered.

"Valuables! Good. Still, what's most important is in your heart," the old lady replied.

Dante giggled. "Hear that, boss?"

The old woman raised an eyebrow at him. "Boss? Maybe you should learn to act on your own. Be a little braver, *m'ijo.*"

Malia was getting a little freaked out by this lady. "Well, uh, thanks! We've got to go."

"There's a shortcut, you know," the woman said. "Turn right before the bakery. The alley's the quickest way to summer fun!"

Dante gave her a thumbs-up. "Thanks, ma'am!"

"Call me Doña Chabela." She pronounced the first word *don-ya*. "I'll see you three on your way back!"

Malia didn't like to take shortcuts. But they were in a hurry.

The alley was behind a bakery and smelled like Mexican pastries. It was shady and cool, but as the kids walked, the sky got darker. When they stepped out of the alley, the wind started to moan and it began to sprinkle.

"No fair!" Dante cried. "What if they close the water park?"

Malia put her arm out to stop them from entering traffic. But there were no cars coming or going. No people crowded the sidewalks. No horns. No voices. No music.

Just eerie silence.

# CHAPTER

3

# NO EXIT, NO ESCAPE

Ivan glanced around the empty street. Most buildings had boarded-up windows. "Is a storm coming?"

Malia pulled her phone from her pink purse. "My weather app says sunny skies."

Dante looked up at the dark clouds. Two drops of rain hit him right in the eyes. "Ugh! Well, your phone's wrong."

Ivan looked worried. "Where's the water park?"

Dante shrugged. "Aunt Lucy said we'd see it when we hit 12th Street."

"Uh-oh," Ivan said, pointing at the street sign. "This is 13th Street!"

Malia squinted. "But we didn't cross any other roads, right?"

"Dunno. We were just following you, boss. As ordered." Dante saluted.

"Maybe the smell of sweet bread distracted her," Ivan said. "She's got a weakness for empanadas."

Malia groaned. "Knock it off, you two. Let's just retrace our steps."

But when they turned to reenter the alley, it was gone!

"Okay," Malia said, trying to stay calm. "Maybe we walked too far away from the entrance."

"We took like three steps, Malia." Dante's voice trembled. "No. Something's not right."

"I'll use my map app to get a better route," Malia said.

But her phone couldn't find their location.

"Could be the storm," Ivan said. "Try looking up the street name."

Malia's thumbs bounced all over the screen. Then, eyes wide, she gave a horrified **GASP**.

"Guys, the map says . . . there is no 13th Street. Not in this town. Not in the **WHOLE STATE!**"

Dante shuddered. "*¡Uy, cucuy!*"

Ivan looked at him funny. "Monster? What monster?"

"No monster, dude. I just say that when I'm freaked out," said Dante.

"Don't talk about monsters, guys," Malia scolded. "It's bad luck!"

Lightning flashed overhead. Thunder shook the ground under their feet.

"Too late," Ivan said.

"Come on!" Malia ordered. "Let's just turn on the first street we find. That should take us back the way we came."

The cousins hurried up the sidewalk. They passed business after business, all closed, windows shuttered.

They jogged a hundred feet. Two hundred. Three hundred. Businesses became apartment buildings. Their windows were dark, their stoops were empty.

There were no other streets. There were no other alleys.

Ivan kicked off his flippers and began to run. Malia and Dante were right behind him. Block after block they ran.

But there was no exit, no escape.

Thirteenth Street went on forever and ever.

# CHAPTER

# SCARY SQUAWKS AND SQUEAKS

Out of breath, the three cousins slowed and stopped.

"This," gasped Dante, "is crazy. Call Aunt Lucy."

Malia nodded, pulling out her phone. But now she had no signal.

"Not good," Ivan muttered.

"Remember what Doña Chabela said," Dante reminded them with a smirk.

"What's most important is in our hearts."

"Gimme a break!" Malia said.

Suddenly Ivan lifted his hand. "Shhh. Do you hear that?"

There was a faint sound in the distance. With the rustling came a creepy clicking and scratching that sent chills down their spines. Then they heard squawks and squeaks echoing all around them.

"What is that?" Dante asked, horrified.

"Sounds like a bunch of birds with broken beaks," Ivan replied.

"And they're getting closer!" Malia pointed out, spinning around and around.

Dante swallowed hard. "Guys, this is really creeping me out!"

The sounds got louder and louder!

# WHOOP! WHOOP!

# CLICK-SCRAAAATCH!

# CLICK-SCRAAAATCH!

# SQUAAAAWWWWK!

# SQUEEEEAAAAK!

The kids
backed up until
their butts
bumped into a
building. Malia
pulled her
floaties down
onto her fists,
lifting them
like a boxer.

That's when
a gigantic
bat dropped
from the sky.

It was **ENORMOUS**! Its leathery
wings were as wide as garbage trucks. Its
thick, stumpy legs ended in shiny sharp claws,
and it had huge pointed ears that could hear
every move of its prey.

# THUD!

The monster landed in the street in front of them.

# SCREEEECH!

It made an earsplitting sound as it slowly turned its head.

Malia wanted to scream. Ivan was ready to run.

Dante's heart was racing. He could hardly move, but he opened his mouth and whispered two words.

"*¡Uy, cucuy!*"

You've read four chapters! ¡Chido! (That means awesome.)

# CHAPTER

# 5

# DESPERATE FOR A DOOR

Malia turned to Dante. "Don't say that again. Do something!"

"L-like w-what?" Dante stuttered. He was so afraid he could barely think.

"I don't know! You've got to be good at *something*!" Malia said.

"Just video games," Ivan muttered.

Something clicked in Dante's brain. Ivan had said the magic words.

"Oh." Dante's eyes got big. "Oh! That's it!"

He turned and looked at the door behind them.

"No, not this one," he said.

The gigantic bat twitched its ears and took a step toward them.

# THUD!

Though his legs were trembling, Dante rushed up the sidewalk a few feet. He stared at the next door. Then he shook his head.

"Not this one, either."

# THUD!

"Dante?" Malia asked, her voice shaky. "Whatever you're doing, hurry!"

Ivan sniffed at the air. "Do you smell that?"

# THUD!

The bat leaned forward, snarling and hissing at them.

Malia gagged. The creature's breath **STANK**!

Ivan dropped to his knees, pinching his nose shut with his fingers.

"That's **DISGUSTING**!" he moaned.

Dante didn't seem to notice. He was squinting, looking across the street, beyond the giant bat. "Maybe?" he said to himself.

Then, over the roofs of the buildings, came hundreds of smaller, people-sized bats.

A wave of wings, claws, and sharp teeth was heading straight for the cousins!

"Dante!" shouted Ivan, looking up. "The stinky monster's got a bunch of friends! Please tell us you found something!"

"I . . . I think so. You know how some

games mark doors you can go through? Like with a green light versus a red one? Well, across the street there are two doors with the exact same symbol. It might mean we can open them."

Malia looked at the buildings Dante was pointing out. On each doorframe was a mark. Two horizontal bars, one on top of the other. Three dots in a line above them.

"Well, maybe we should . . . ," Malia began. Then something grabbed at her hair!

Twisting around, she saw bats climbing down the front of the building! One of them hooked its claws in her curls. It was trying to yank her into the air! Nasty bat breath spilled all over her.

Malia pulled away and rushed into the street with a scream. "Run!"

Ivan hurried after her. The bats launched themselves into the air.

"Oh, Dante, you'd better be right!" Ivan shouted. They all raced toward the nearest marked door.

Malia reached it first. A dozen bats

swooped toward her! They opened their nasty jaws. The odor was almost too much!

Malia held her breath, grabbed the doorknob, and turned.

There was a click. Malia yanked the door open.

Just then, Ivan and Dante slammed into her from behind!

The three cousins went tumbling into the darkness inside.

# CHAPTER

# A GHOSTLY HOST

"Oh no! You're going to let them in!"

It was a girl's voice. She sounded worried.

With good reason. The gigantic bat's face was looming just outside the door!

"Close up, Kalaan!" the girl shouted.

The door slammed shut.

The cousins had tumbled to the floor. Malia stood up and flipped the light switch near the closed door.

They were in a lobby. Standing at the foot of the stairs was a girl.

And she was transparent. Malia could literally see the staircase *through* the outline of the girl's body.

Malia shuddered and squeezed her yellow duck. The air blew out with a squeak. The girl giggled.

"A ghost!" Dante said. He sat up and crossed himself.

"Hmm . . . I don't *think* I'm a ghost," the girl said. "I don't *feel* dead, anyway."

Ivan was still on the floor. "Well, you sure are see-through. And," he added, putting his cheek against the tile, "whoa, and your feet aren't touching the ground."

"My name is Yoliya," the girl said. "And you're lucky you got away from the Snatch Bats when you did."

Ivan sat up. "I'm Ivan, and that's Malia and Dante."

The girl smiled, like she was happy to have company.

"What was that thing you said?" Ivan asked. "'Close up, Kalaan.' Is that the reverse of 'open sesame' or something?"

Yoliya nodded. "Yes, more or less. Except to open a door, we say, 'Open, Hebaan.' Uh-oh!"

**WHAM!** The door opened.

Dozens of Snatch Bats screeched and zoomed toward them.

Malia jumped back, startled. Then she reached out and slammed the door shut before the monsters could get inside.

"Okaaaay," Malia said. "Look, we're not from here. We got lost."

"I'm not from here, either," Yoliya said, tears forming in her eyes. "I . . . don't remember *where* I'm from."

"Does anyone else live here?" Ivan asked.

Yoliya sniffled. "Not in this building. I do have neighbors, though, who—"

"But can you help us escape?" Malia interrupted.

"There's only one way off 13th Street," Yoliya said. "Defeat the threat. Then a portal back to your world will open."

"Ah!" Dante exclaimed. "We have to level up!"

YES! You just read two more chapters—even with bats chasing you!

# CHAPTER

# ROOFTOP RUN

"Defeat them? That's crazy! We're just three kids," Malia said. "They're . . . like, huge flying rats!"

Ivan stood. "We don't have any weapons. I even lost my flippers running from those bad-breath bats."

Dante gave a nervous laugh. "I don't think it would have helped."

Yoliya smiled. "That's why you have to go to the Depot of the Dead."

Dante gulped. Ivan's eyes opened wide.

Malia sighed. "Doesn't sound like a place we want to visit."

"The storekeeper has lots of amazing things on his shelves," Yoliya explained. "I'm sure you can find something to fight the Snatch Bats with."

Dante snapped his fingers. "Just like a video game. We go in, find what we need."

Ivan nodded. "Then we buy it!"

Malia shook her head. "We don't have any money."

"Okay, then we . . . trade for it!" Ivan said.

"Trade what? Your snorkel?" Malia asked.

Yoliya interrupted. "Just tell him I sent you. He'll make a deal."

Malia turned to the door and looked through the peephole.

The Snatch Bats were flying around outside. Waiting.

"Tell me there's another way to this . . . Depot of the Dead," Malia said.

Yoliya shrugged. "I just walk through the walls."

Malia rolled her eyes. "Not an option."

"Is there a back door?" Dante asked.

"No," said Yoliya. "But you can go to the roof. The depot's only three buildings down. You can jump from roof to roof!"

"But the bats might attack!" Dante complained.

"They won't expect us up there," Ivan promised.

Yoliya rushed up the stairs. Ivan and Malia followed. The choice was made.

There were three floors, and then a few more steps to the roof.

The cousins stood under the gloomy sky. It was filled with a dark mist.

"Okay," Yoliya said, standing nearby. "It was good meeting you. I hope you make it out. If not, come visit me. It gets lonely here."

The door shut. It had the same strange symbol as the front entrance.

The cousins reached the edge of the roof. The next roof was pressed right against it. No gap. But it was a little lower. They climbed quietly over the edge and dropped to the flat, dirty surface of the second roof.

A Snatch Bat popped through the strange gray sky. Right out of thin air!

It saw them and screeched!

The other creatures must have heard, because the air was suddenly filled with the sound of beating wings.

# WHOOP! WHOOP!

The cousins ran like they had never run before!

# AAARRRRK!

The Snatch Bats rose into the air behind them!

Ivan tripped over his own feet, but Dante caught him. They kept running.

The creatures were getting closer.

The next building was taller. Malia looked down at the deflated yellow duck in her hands. It had cost her parents a lot of money. She really, really loved it.

"What are you doing, Malia?" Ivan shouted. "They're coming!"

Closing her eyes for a second, Malia tossed the plastic aside. She jumped and grabbed the edge of the roof. Ivan gave her a boost, then helped Dante up, too.

The Snatch Bats dived toward him!

Ivan was tall enough to reach the roof. He pulled himself up. His cousins were rushing to a door with the mysterious symbol.

Just as Ivan started to run toward them, he was yanked into the air by one of the bats!

# CHAPTER

8

# STRANGE STOREKEEPER

The big bat glared at Ivan. Its lips curled back, revealing teeth like knives. Then its breath hit. The stink was powerful. Ivan found it hard to move.

But as the creature opened its jaws, Ivan lifted his right hand. He ripped his snorkel from his mask. Then he shoved it into the bat's mouth!

With a roar of pain, the monster let him go.

Ivan landed on the roof and limped toward his cousins.

They were yanking on the door, desperate.

"It's stuck!" cried Dante.

Ivan shook his head, sighing. He shouted, "Open, Hebaan!"

The door popped open. Malia and Dante hurried inside. Ivan was right behind them.

"Close up, Kalaan!" he said, just as the Snatch Bats came flying toward them.

# WHOOSH!
# SLAM!

The bats couldn't stop themselves. One by one they smashed into the closed door!

# BOOM! BAM! BASH!

"Downstairs," said Malia.

At the second landing, there was a man standing in a large doorway. His back was to them. At the sound of their heavy breathing, he turned around.

Dante let out a frightened squeak.

"AH! It's a *calavera*!"

The man was indeed a skeleton! Not a scary one, though. He had friendly eyes. "*¡Hola!* I'm Omi, the storekeeper."

Ivan knew it was impossible. Skeletons couldn't talk.

But maybe anything was possible on 13th Street.

"H-hello," Malia stuttered. "Yoliya sent us. We need to defeat the Snatch Bats."

"Well, step into the depot, *chamacos*, and take a look around!" Omi said cheerfully.

# CHAPTER

9

# DEPOT OF THE DEAD

They followed Omi inside. His bones made weird marimba sounds as he walked.

The Depot of the Dead was a big showroom. Lining the walls were many shelves covered with different items.

Plus dust.

And cobwebs.

"Let's split up," Ivan suggested.

"Um, you can check that side," Dante said, his voice still a little shaky. "Me and Malia will look over here."

Most of the things on the shelves were silly or useless. Tennis rackets with no strings. Chipped coffee cups. Unmatched left shoes. Blankets with holes.

"Look!" Dante had grabbed a large water gun. Two more were on a shelf nearby.

"Water won't stop them," Malia said.

Omi was with Ivan. He had a huge smile.

"How do you defeat Snatch Bats?" Ivan asked.

"No idea. I wouldn't try it," Omi replied.

Ivan scratched his head. "A skeleton. A ghost girl. Are we . . . dead?"

The storekeeper poked him in the chest with a bony finger.

"Ow!" Ivan complained.

"Nope, not dead," Omi said.

Malia stormed over, upset. "This is *everything* you have in stock?"

Omi shook his head. "Oh, no, *m'ijita*. There's more in the storeroom. Follow me."

They went down to the basement. Omi showed them a much bigger room, stuffed with boxes and crates.

Arranged in the middle were hundreds of bottles of blue-green liquid.

Ivan snapped his fingers.

"Yes! Mouthwash," he said. "We'll take all of it."

Nine chapters down! *¡Adelante!* (That means *keep going!*)

# CHAPTER

# 10

# SWEET-SMELLING STRATEGY

Malia narrowed her eyes. "What?"

Ivan explained. "These bats' nasty breath freezes muscles up. Mouthwash should take that power away."

Dante nodded. "Smart!"

Malia crossed her arms. "And how are we supposed to get it in their mouths, genius?"

Dante answered before Ivan could. "We fill up those water guns, and . . ."

"Squirt!" Ivan finished. "Minty-fresh victory."

"*Momentito*," said Omi, lifting up his bony hand. "Time to haggle."

"Excuse me?" Dante asked.

The skeleton rubbed his fingers together: squeak, squeak. "Payment. What've you got to swap?"

smartphone

hairbrush

bubblegum lip balm

cat ear barrettes

sunglasses

They laid out all of their belongings on top of a box of toilet paper, including Malia's purse and everything in it.

"These will do just fine," said Omi, gathering the items up.

Malia's eyes watered. Her parents had bought her the little handbag as a reward for good grades and behavior. It wasn't fair!

"Boss," Dante warned. "We need this trade."

"Fine. It's a deal," Malia said with a sigh. Their freedom was more important than her possessions.

But she refused to shake the shopkeeper's hand.

There were limits, after all!

# CHAPTER

# BEATING THE BATS

Ten minutes later, the front door to the Depot of the Dead burst open. Out walked Malia Malapata, Dante Dávila, and Ivan Eisenberg.

Each of them was holding a huge water gun loaded with mouthwash as a swarm of Snatch Bats swirled around them.

"Now!" shouted Malia.

She pulled the trigger when one of the Snatch Bats lurched toward her. It was screeching. The stream of mouthwash went right into its mouth.

The bat stopped in its tracks. Its red eyes went wide. Foam dribbled from its jaws.

Then it dropped to the ground, twitching.

All at once, the rest of the bats launched toward the cousins!

Dante raised his water gun and started squirting. "Aim for their mouths!"

# SQUISH! SQUISH!

Dante and Malia took out six of the monsters in just a few seconds.

Ivan, however, was having problems. His aim wasn't good. He kept splashing the bats in the eyes, which just made them madder.

"You have to adjust for your terrible aim!" Malia yelled. "Point at their chests, Ivan!"

Her order didn't make much sense, but Ivan was too nervous to argue. A bat was swooping toward him. He aimed for its chest.

# SQUISH!

He hit it right in the mouth!

"Wow, boss!" Dante said between blasts. "You're good at this!"

"My mom taught me," Malia explained. "She learned in the Marine Corps."

After that, there was no time for talking. Wave after wave of bats kept coming.

Malia's water gun ran out first. She rushed back to the building.

"Storekeeper! Reload!"

The door opened, and the colorful *calavera* tossed her another bottle. She uncapped it and quickly refilled her weapon.

"Don't move. The boys will need more soon."

After thirty minutes of fighting, there were just a couple of bats still flying. The rest were in heaps on the ground.

"We're going to level up soon!" Dante said with a happy laugh.

Then the ground started to tremble. A shadow fell on them.

Dante gulped. "After we beat the Boss Bat, I mean."

# CHAPTER

# BOSS BATTLE

The cousins looked up. The Boss Bat stood with its wings spread wide. It opened its horrible jaws and blew a nasty stench at them!

"Hang on!" Malia called as Ivan's and Dante's knees buckled. "Remember the plan!"

"You got it!" Dante said, gagging. "*Ghostbusters* style!"

The three of them lifted their water guns,

ready to fire at once and cross their minty-fresh streams.

But the massive monster swung its wing tip at them. A single claw ripped through their weapons, smashing them to little bits!

# SCREECH!

Strings of saliva flew from its mouth. The cousins fled in different directions.

Ivan rolled under a rusted car. Howling, the giant creature grabbed the vehicle with one clawed foot and threw it into a nearby building. Ivan ran off and the other bats followed.

Dante squeezed into a narrow space between two buildings on the other side of the street. He hid behind some moss-covered trash cans. The Boss Bat saw him and went charging at the gap.

# WHAM!
# CRACK!

It beat its head against the two buildings. Bricks came loose, showering down on

Dante. He grabbed a trash can lid and used it as a shield.

The other bats caught up to Ivan. Each one grabbed an arm.

Malia ran back to the Depot of the Dead for another bottle. She knew there was just one option. She had to save the day.

# CHAPTER

# MALIA AND THE MOUTHWASH

Malia climbed onto the roof of the truck.

"Hey, stinkface!" she shouted, loosening the bottle cap.

The giant Snatch Bat turned and saw Malia. It stomped toward her. Malia swung the bottle back and forth. She was going to throw it like a water balloon as soon as the monster got close enough.

But before she could do that, the Boss Bat stretched out a leg . . .

. . . **AND GRABBED HER IN ITS CLAWS**!

Her arms were pinned to her body! She could hardly move!

The Boss Bat lifted Malia toward its **YAWNING JAWS**. Its teeth and tongue were covered with pink slime. The stench was **TOO MUCH**!

The bottle was still in Malia's right hand. It poked up above the bat's thick toes. And she could still move her neck!

Below, Dante came running into the street. "Leave her alone!"

"Get back, Dante!" Malia shouted. "I got this!"

She bent her head. Using her teeth, she grabbed the bottle. Tilting her head back, she let the minty-fresh liquid fill her mouth till her cheeks hurt.

The Boss Bat's snarling face was just inches away!

Before it could eat her, Malia managed to spit out the mouthwash . . .

. . . right into the monster's jaws!

# SPLASH!

It gave a horrible **SCREEEEECH**! Stumbling backward, it dropped Malia to the sidewalk.

Then it toppled over like a rotten old tree.

# TIMBER!
# WHAM!

You've read thirteen chapters! And the bats LOST—hooray!

# CHAPTER

# EXIT AND ESCAPE

"That was **AMAZING**, boss!" Dante shouted as he tossed aside the trash can lid. "Are you okay?"

"Yeah," Malia said as he helped her stand. "Thanks."

"Look, guys!"

It was Ivan, running toward them. Everywhere, the bats were shrinking.

In seconds they were normal size. Malia spun around. The Boss Bat had shrunk down, too!

"Your plan worked, Ivan!" she said.

"*Our* plan, Malia," Ivan corrected. "Without Dante's video game skills and your leadership . . ."

"Don't get all mushy on me," she said. But her eyes teared up.

The door to the depot opened. Omi walked out. Behind him floated Yoliya.

"Hey!" Malia shouted. "You said that a portal would open up!"

Suddenly, all the bats leaped into the air! With tiny squeaks, they flew off toward the sky.

They left a minty-fresh scent behind.

Yoliya shrugged. "I don't understand. They're all gone. The portal should appear."

They heard a screech and looked up. One last bat was flying away into the sky. Once it disappeared, a glowing circle opened in the air in front of the cousins. Inside it, Malia could see the entrance to the alley.

"Hurry!" Yoliya said. "It closes fast!"

Dante and Ivan rushed right through the portal.

Malia turned to the skeleton and the ghost girl.

"You could come with us."

The storekeeper shook his head. "No. Not now, anyway."

Yoliya's eyes filled with tears. "Go!"

As Malia hurried back to her own world, she heard an unfamiliar voice whisper:

"First checkpoint, children."

# CHAPTER

15

# GAME OVER?

The cousins wasted no time. They ran back up the alley, ignoring the sweet smell of pastries. When they reached 11th Street, they turned, heading toward their aunt's apartment building.

Malia slowed as they passed the house of Doña Chabela. There was no sign of the old woman.

"I wonder if she knew," Dante said.

"It's pretty suspicious," Ivan agreed.

Malia clenched her hands into fists. She stomped right up to Doña Chabela's front door and pounded with all her might.

No one answered.

"Forget about it, boss." Dante had come up behind her. He touched her arm gently. "Let's just go home."

As the three kids walked away, a face appeared at a window. It was a woman, watching their backs with a hopeful smile.

Doña Chabela.

The cousins didn't see her, though. They were distracted by the sudden appearance of Aunt Lucy. She came running up the street toward them.

"*¡Ay, pingos!*" she exclaimed. "You almost gave me a heart attack! I've been calling and calling. I went down to the water park and you weren't there! And what **HAPPENED** to you? You're all dirty and scratched up!"

Malia opened her mouth to tell Aunt Lucy

everything, but Ivan spoke first.

"We took a shortcut through the alley. Some bullies jumped us. They stole Malia's phone. We chased them, but they got away.

We were lost for a while."

Dante and Malia stared at him. He never lied. They were amazed how good he was at it. He must have thought Aunt Lucy wouldn't believe the truth anyway! Besides, she was worried enough.

"The good thing is that you're back and you're okay," Aunt Lucy said, reaching out to hug them.

She was quite surprised at how tightly they kept clinging to her.

"*Ya, ya,*" she muttered, patting their heads. "I love you, too. Now . . . how about a video game?"

The three cousins pulled away from her embrace.

"No!" they said all at once.

Then they looked at each other and laughed.

That's the end...for now!

# ACTIVITIES

## THINK!

In the story, Malia doesn't want to give Omi her purse. On a piece of paper, draw the one thing inside your backpack you don't ever want to give up.

## FEEL!

Think of a moment when you were surprised. What did you do to get back on track? Tell your story to a friend or write about it in your journal!

## ACT!

The cousins work together to escape 13th Street. What can you do with your friends to help people in your community? Write down your ideas and circle your favorites.

**DAVID BOWLES** is the award-winning Mexican American author of many books for young readers. He's traveled all over Mexico studying creepy legends, exploring ancient ruins, and avoiding monsters (so far). He lives in Donna, Texas.

**SHANE CLESTER** has been a professional illustrator since 2005, working on comics, storyboards, and children's books. Shane lives in Florida with his wonderful wife and their two tots. When not illustrating, he can usually be found by the pool.